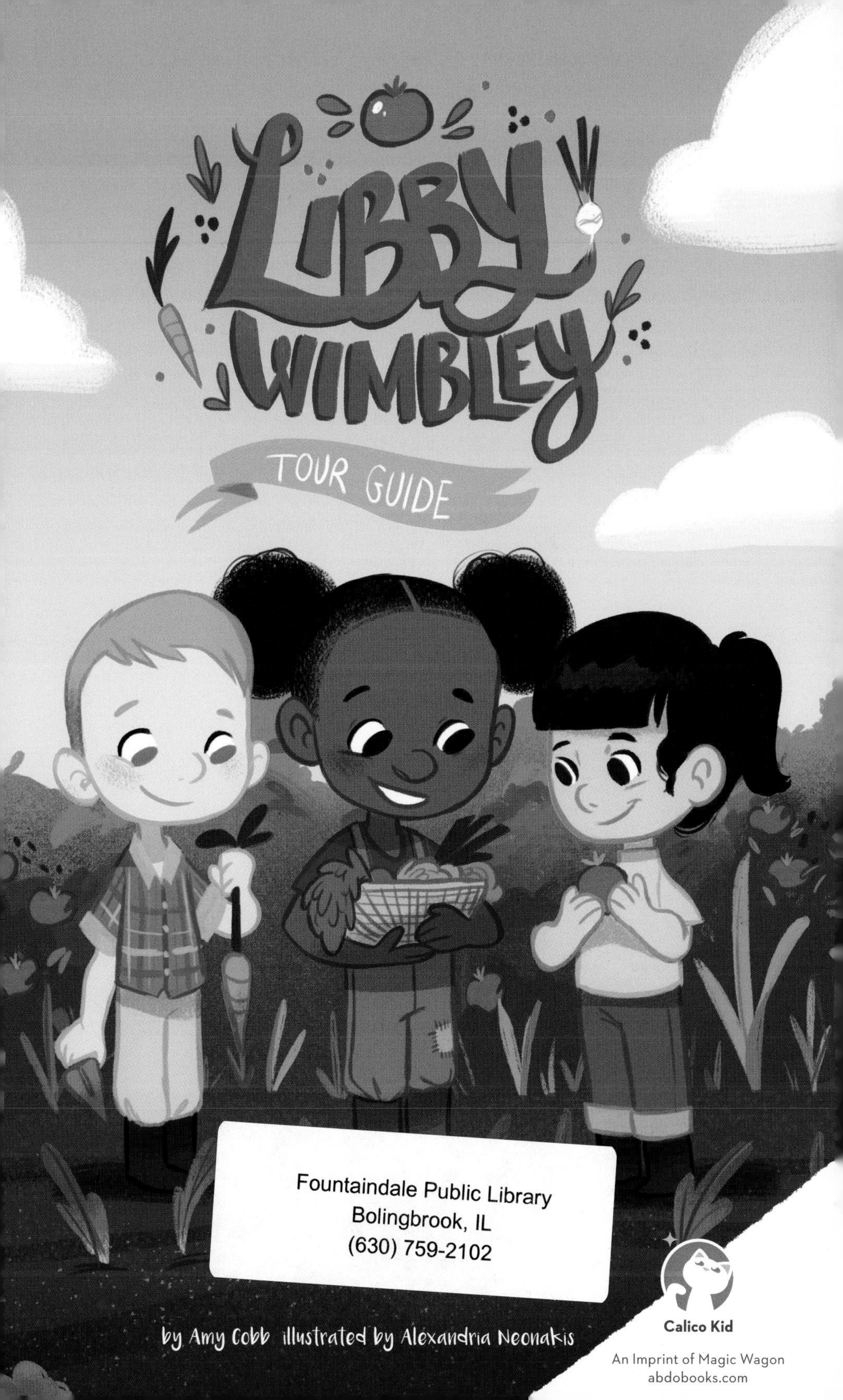
Libby Wimbley
TOUR GUIDE
by Amy Cobb illustrated by Alexandria Neonakis
Calico Kid
An Imprint of Magic Wagon
abdobooks.com

With gratitude to my Creator —AC

To John, Kitty and Gooby for their constant love and support. —AN

abdobooks.com

Published by Magic Wagon, a division of ABDO, PO Box 398166, Minneapolis, Minnesota 55439. Copyright © 2019 by Abdo Consulting Group, Inc. International copyrights reserved in all countries. No part of this book may be reproduced in any form without written permission from the publisher. Calico Kid™ is a trademark and logo of Magic Wagon.

Printed in the United States of America, North Mankato, Minnesota.
102018
012019

Written by Amy Cobb
Illustrated by Alexandria Neonakis
Edited by Tamara L. Britton
Art Directed by Laura Mitchell

Library of Congress Control Number: 2018931808

Publisher's Cataloging-in-Publication Data

Names: Cobb, Amy, author. | Neonakis, Alexandria, illustrator.
Title: Tour guide / by Amy Cobb; illustrated by Alexandria Neonakis.
Description: Minneapolis, Minnesota : Magic Wagon, 2019. | Series: Libby Wimbley set 2
Summary: Libby can't believe it when she finds out some of the other kids at summer camp
    have never visited a farm! So she invites them over for a farm tour. Libby even plans an
    outdoor picnic with farm-to-table snacks.
Identifiers: ISBN 9781532132551 (lib.bdg.) | ISBN 9781532132759 (ebook) |
    ISBN 9781532132858 (Read-to-me ebook)
Subjects: LCSH: Summer camps—Juvenile fiction. | Farms—Juvenile fiction. |
    Tourism—Juvenile fiction. | Farm life—Juvenile fiction. | Friendship—Juvenile fiction.
Classification: DDC [FIC]—dc23

Table of Contents

Chapter #1
Show-and-Tell

Each summer, Libby Wimbley went to Reading Camp at the library. Today's theme was show-and-tell. Libby couldn't wait to see what everyone brought to share.

"Who wants to go first?" asked Mrs. King, the librarian.

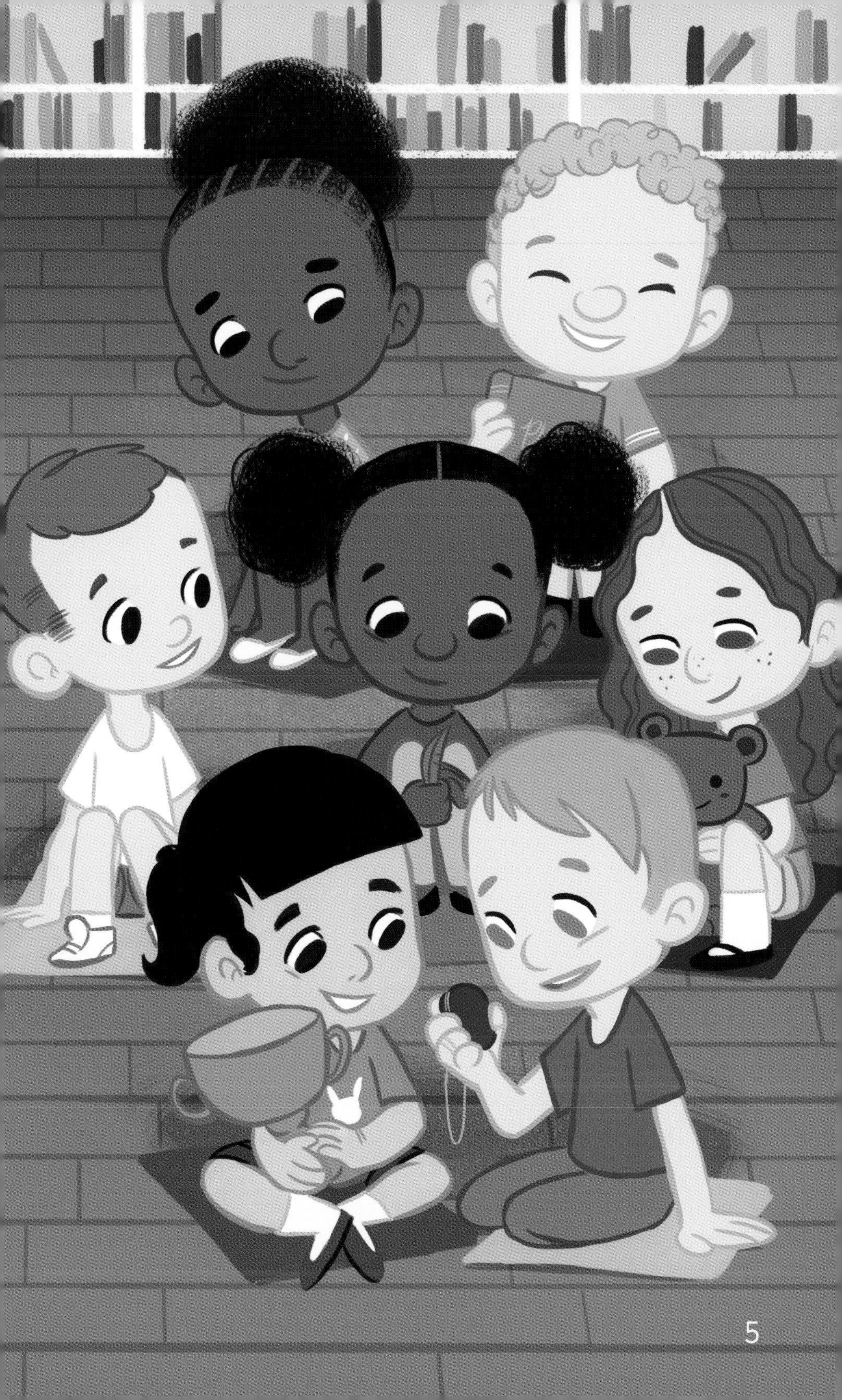

"Me!" shouted Alex. "I brought a yo-yo."

Everyone clapped when Alex did a cool trick.

"Check out my trophy," said Xuni. "My painting won first place."

The kids clapped for Xuni, too.

"Your turn, Libby," Mrs. King said.

But suddenly, Libby didn't want to show. Or tell. She didn't have a fun trick. She didn't have a fancy prize she'd won either.

"Come on, Libby!" Clark said. "Let's see what you brought."

"Libby will show us when she's ready," Mrs. King said.

Libby didn't think she'd ever be ready. But she took a deep breath. Then finally, she showed everyone what she'd brought.

"A bird feather?" asked Xuni.

Libby nodded. "It's a Doodle feather."

"What's a Doodle?" Alex asked.

Libby smiled. "Doodle's my rooster. He lives on our farm."

"Wow!" Clark said. "I've never been to a farm."

"Me neither," said Xuni.

"Next time," said Alex, "bring Doodle for show-and-tell."

Mrs. King shook her head. "Roosters don't have library cards."

Everyone laughed.

But Libby thought about it. Maybe the kids could meet Doodle. Somehow.

Chapter #2
Guess What?

On the way home from the library that afternoon, Libby told Mom all about show-and-tell. "Alex did a yo-yo trick called the UFO. And Xuni's first place trophy was awesome."

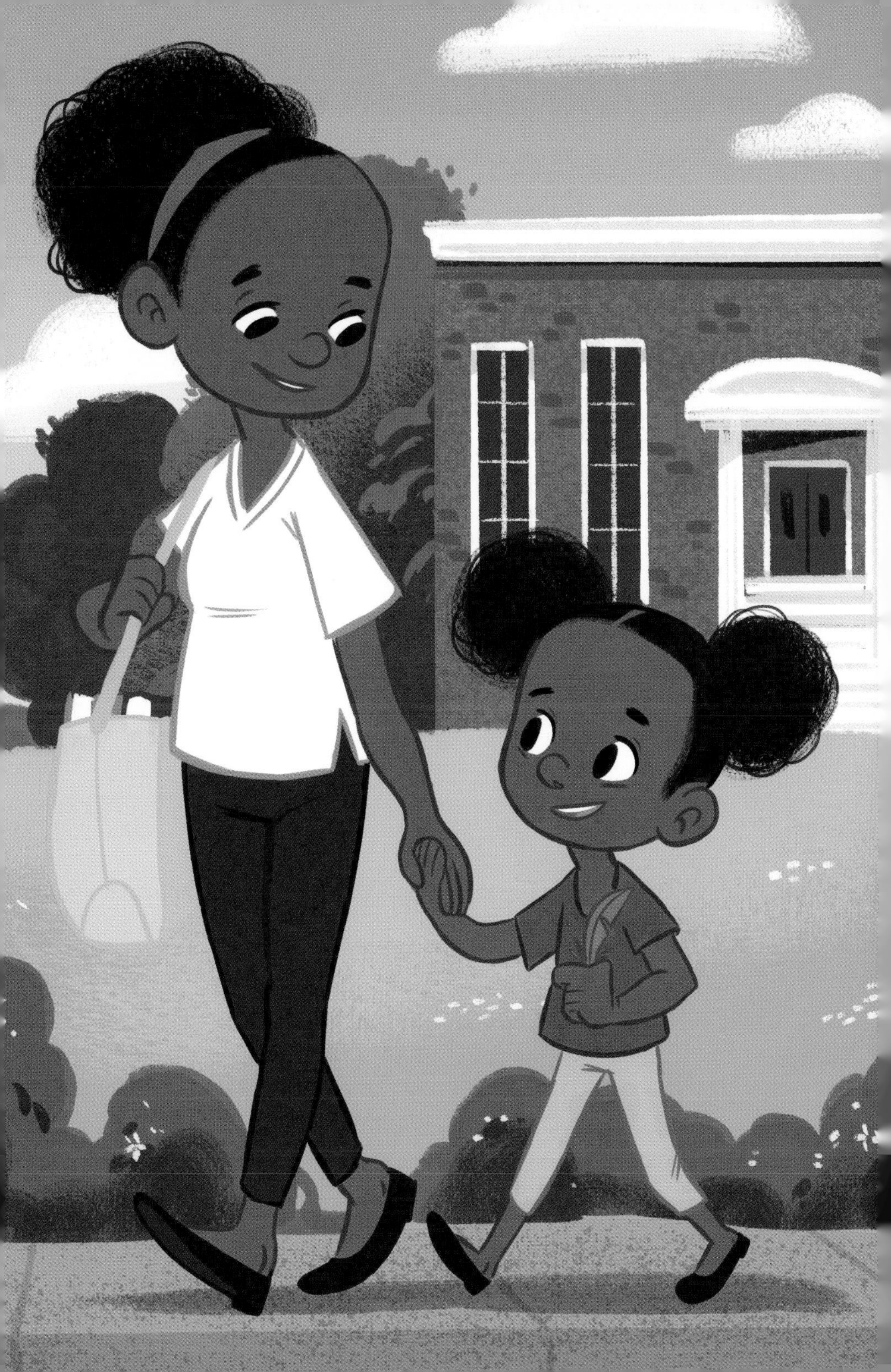

Mom nodded. "How did everyone like Doodle's feather you took to share?"

"They thought it was really soft. And tickly!" Libby said. "But guess what?"

"What?" Mom asked.

"Clark and Xuni have never been to a farm before!"

"Well," Mom began, "everyone doesn't get the chance to visit a farm, Libby."

That made Libby sad. She thought everyone should see all of the farm animals. And pick vegetables from a garden. Mrs. King said Doodle couldn't come to the library. But what if the library came to the farm?

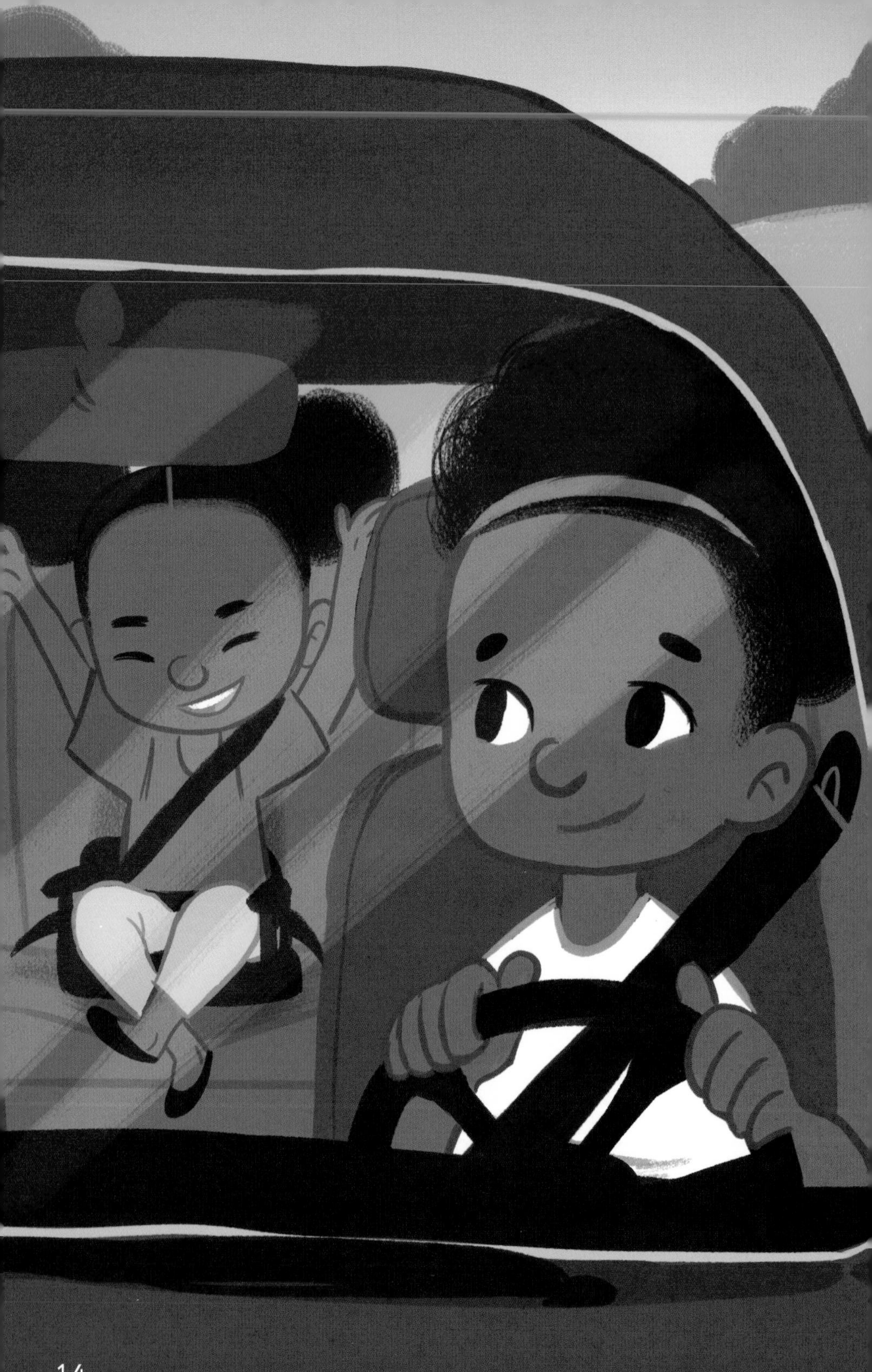

"That's it!" Libby said. "Let's invite the kids from the library over to our farm."

Mom parked the car. "You mean, like a field trip?"

"Exactly!" Libby smiled.

"That sounds fun," Mom said.

Libby thought so, too.

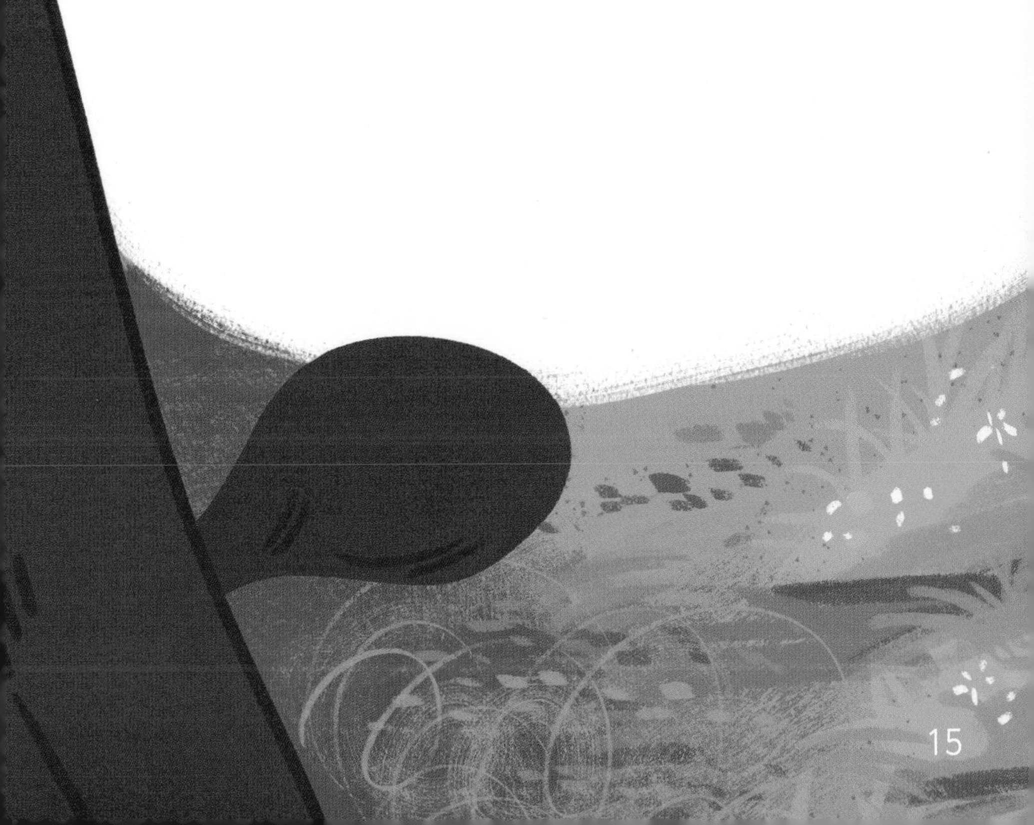

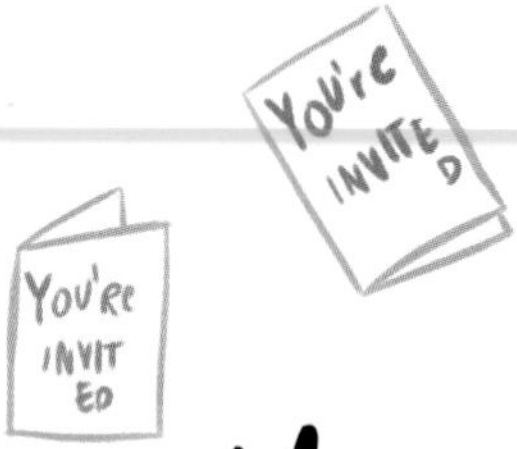
You're INVIT ED
You're INVITE D

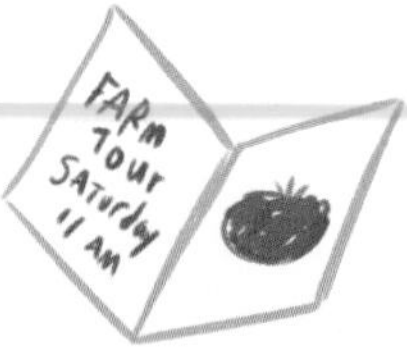
FARM Tour SATurday 11 AM

Chapter #3

You're Invited!

At Reading Camp the next week, Libby passed out invitations she'd made.

"You're invited to Libby's Fun on the Farm Tour!" Xuni read. Then she smiled. "Thank you, Libby. I'd love to come!"

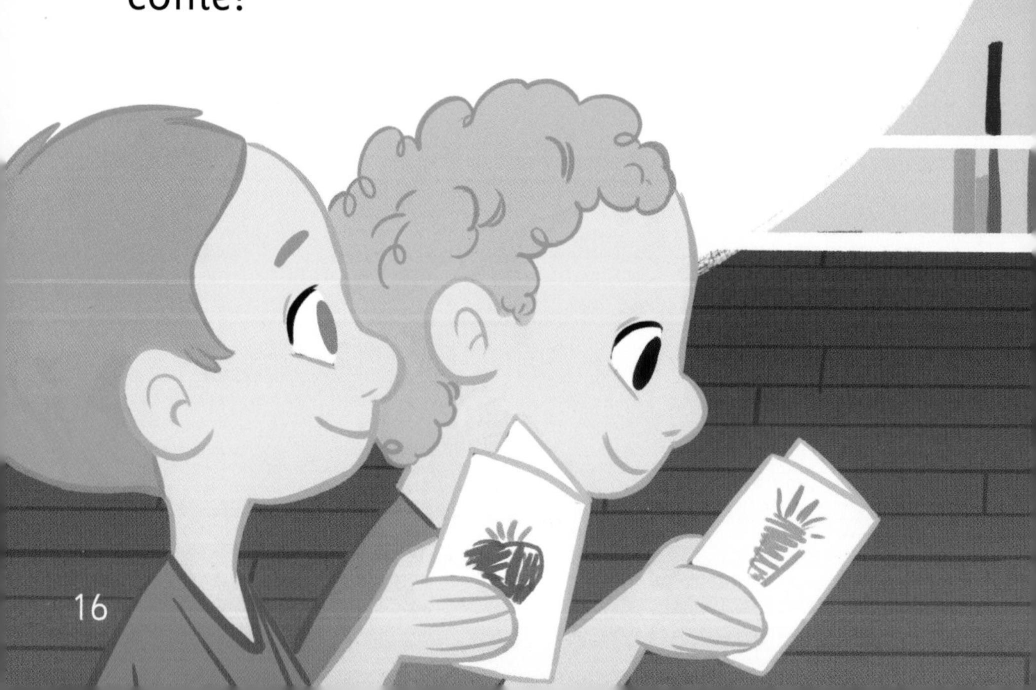

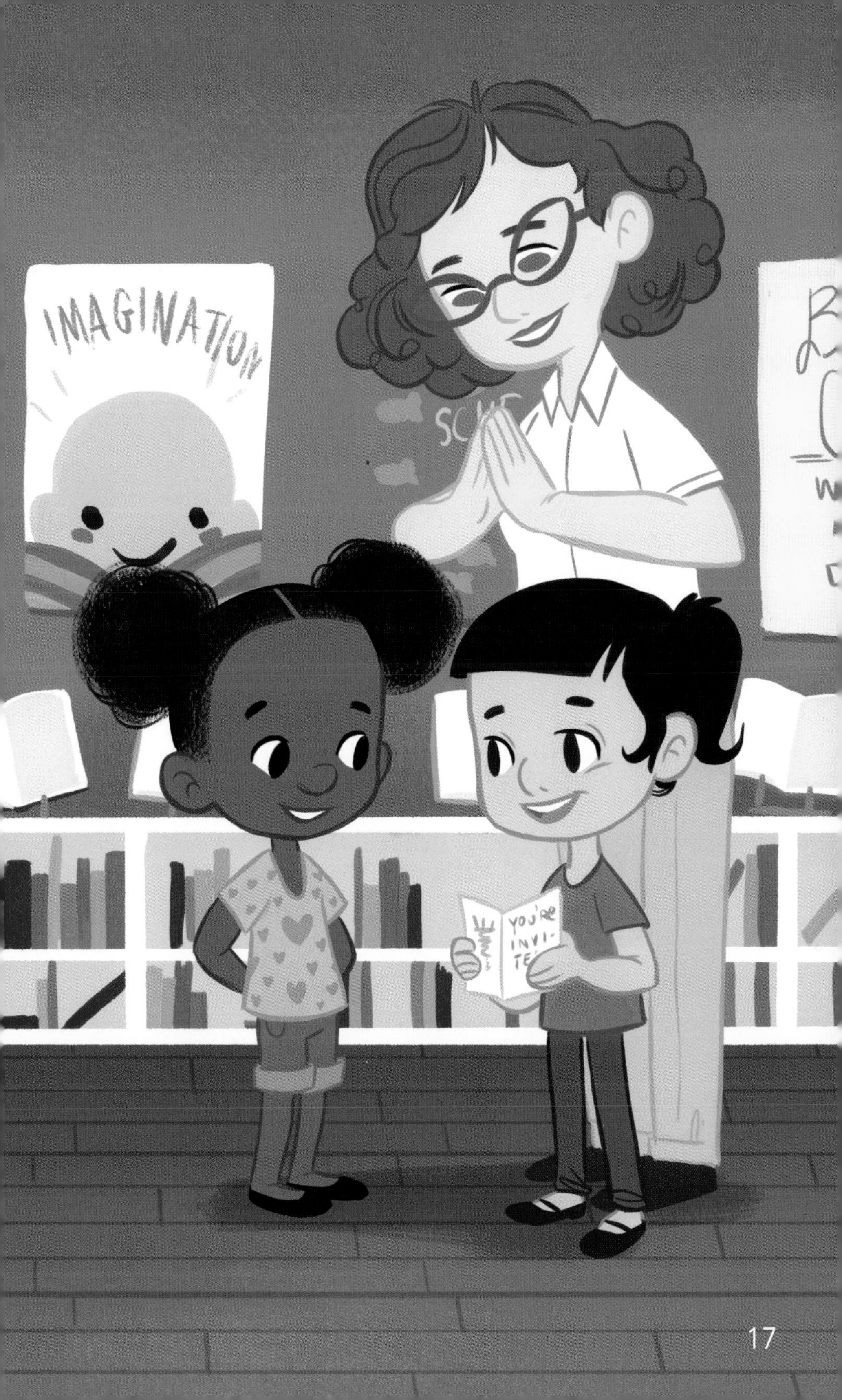
IMAGINATION
YOU'RE INVI-TE

"Me too!" said Clark.

Alex said he'd come, too. So did lots of other kids. And even Mrs. King.

But now that everyone was coming out to the farm the next day, Libby had a lot of work to do.

First, Libby brushed the cows and pony. She even gave her goat, Elvis, a bath. "You look beautiful, Elvis!"

"Meh-meh!" Elvis said.

Later on, Libby swept the barn. She cleaned out the henhouse. Then Libby and Dad set up a hay bale maze in the backyard.

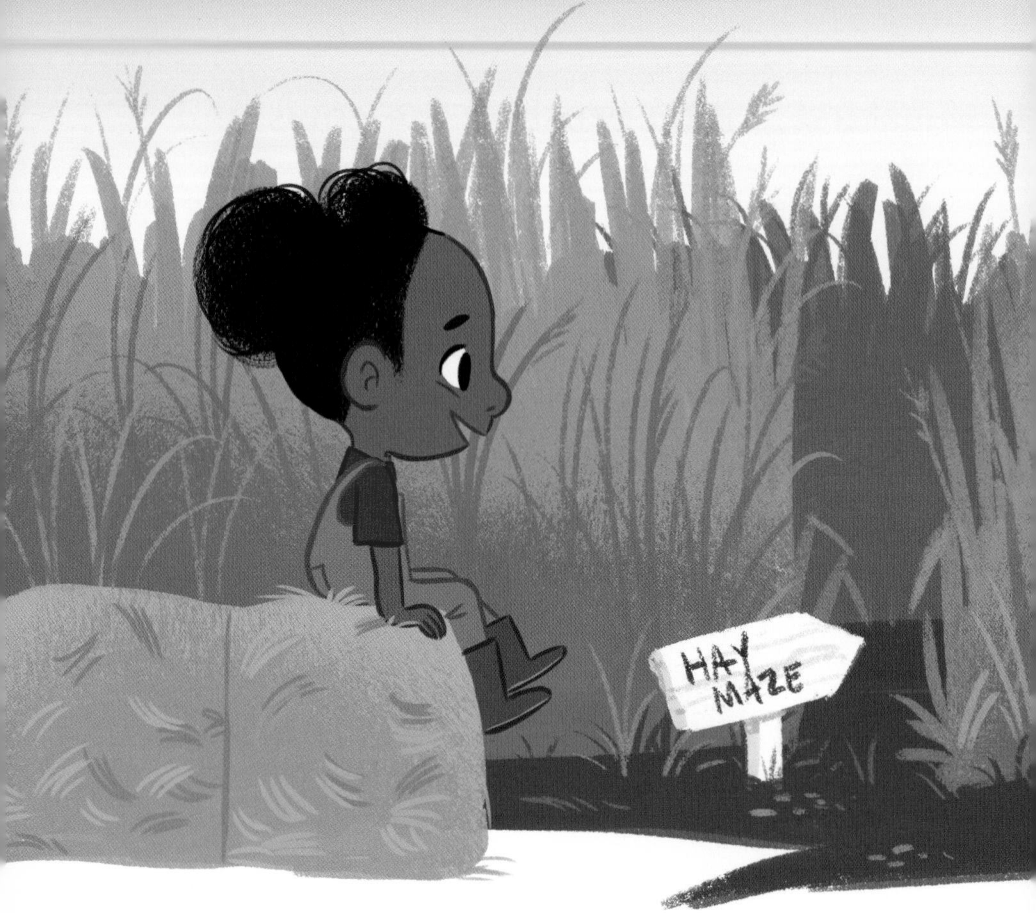
HAY
MAZE

When they were finished, Libby stopped to rest. "You know, being a farmer is hard work," she said.

"Really?" Dad made a surprised face.

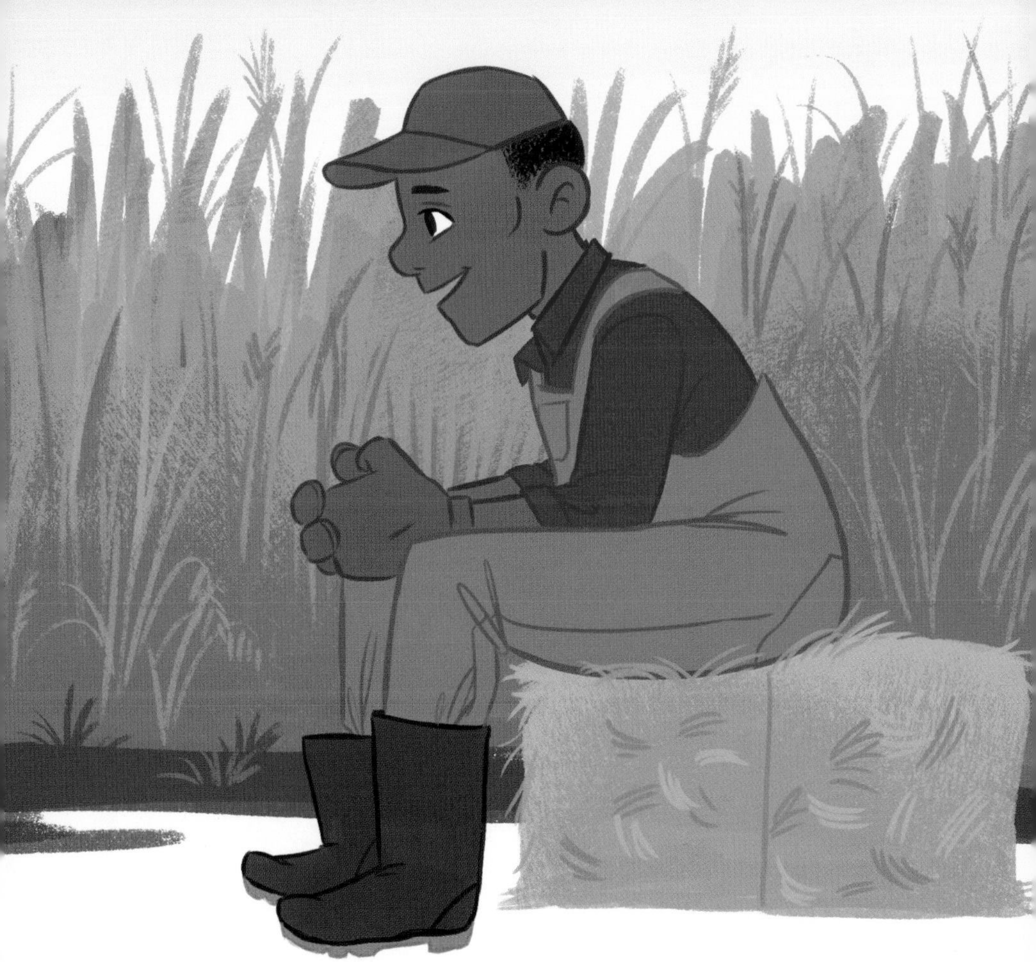

“Really!” Libby laughed.

Even though Libby was tired, she was excited about her friends visiting the farm tomorrow.

Chapter #4

An Egg-citing Afternoon

"Welcome to our farm," Libby said. "Come meet our animals."

She led Mrs. King, Alex, Xuni, Clark, and the other kids from Reading Camp to the pasture.

There, the cows and pony rested beneath shade trees. In another field, the goats munched on grass. One goat came over to be petted.

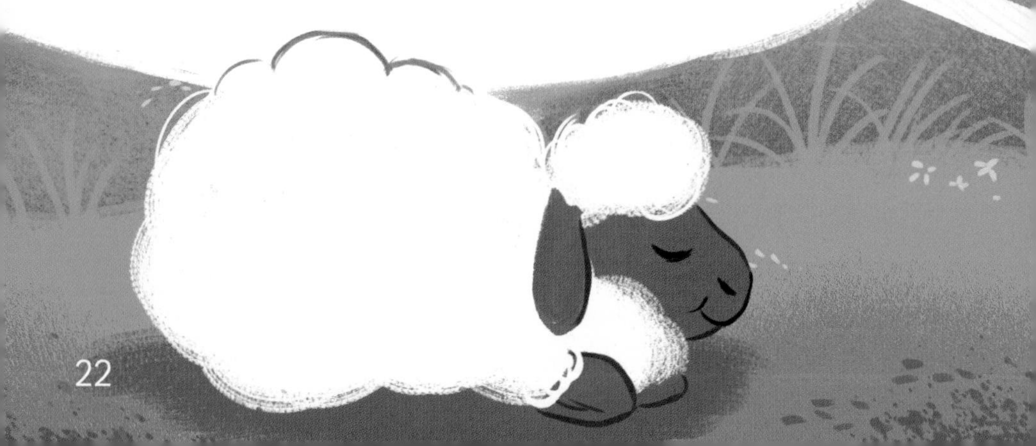

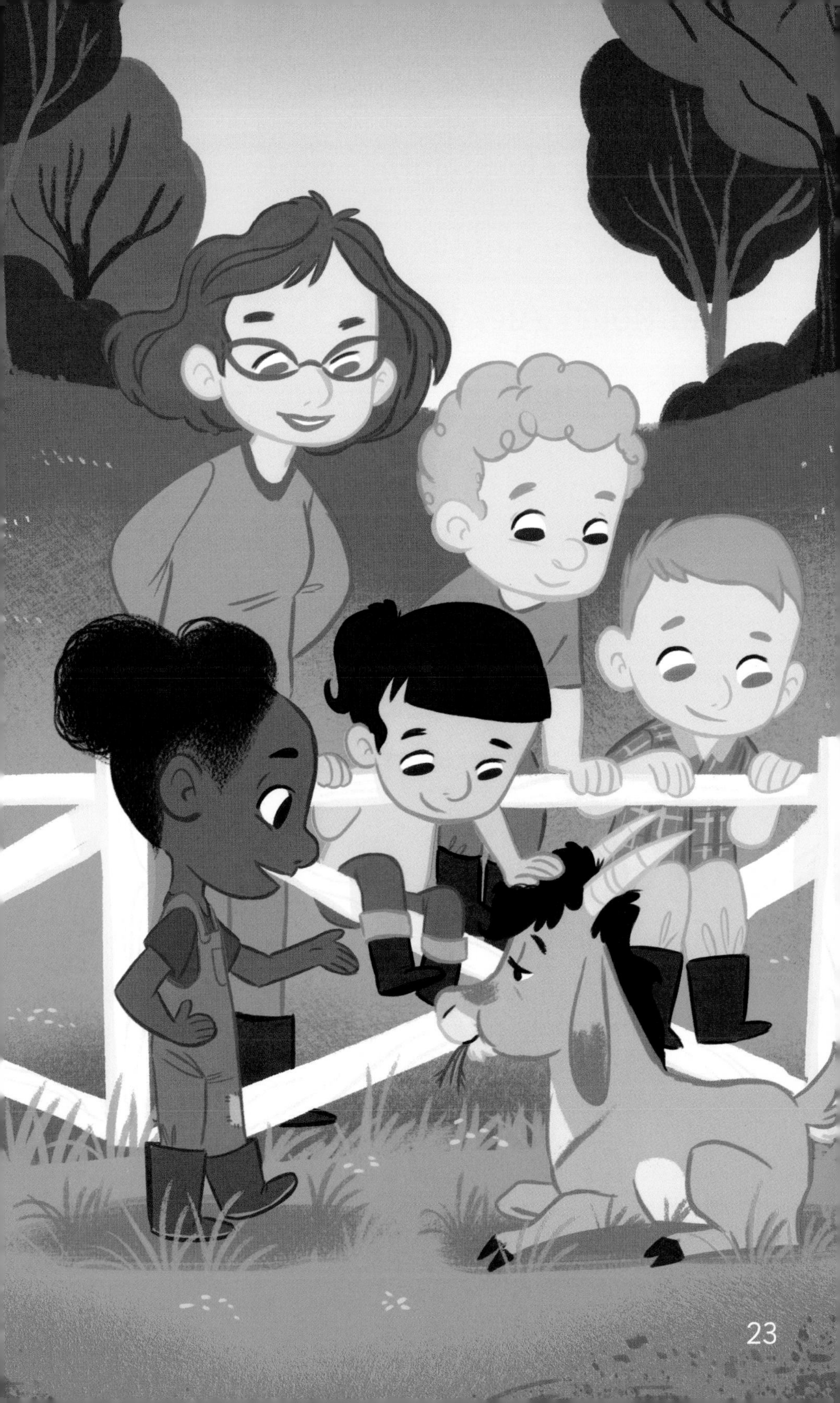

"This is Elvis," Libby said.

"Does he sing like the King of Rock and Roll?" Alex joked.

"Meh-meh!" Elvis sang.

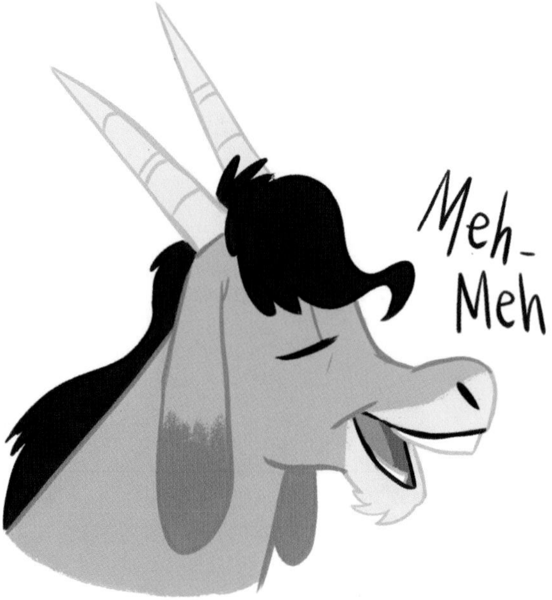
Meh-
Meh

Everyone laughed.

Inside the barn, the kids saw some pigs and chickens.

"Who'd like to gather eggs from the hens?" Libby asked.

"I want to!" Xuni said.

Clark said, "So do I!"

"Let's go!" Libby grabbed a basket.

Everyone took turns reaching into the nests and pulling out eggs.

"What'll we do with all of these eggs?" Alex asked.

Libby handed the basket to Mom and smiled. "You'll see."

"Hey!" Clark said. "Where's Doodle?"

"Right there." Libby pointed to a fence post.

Doodle fluffed his feathers. "Cock-a-doodle-doo!"

Everyone tried crowing, just like Doodle.

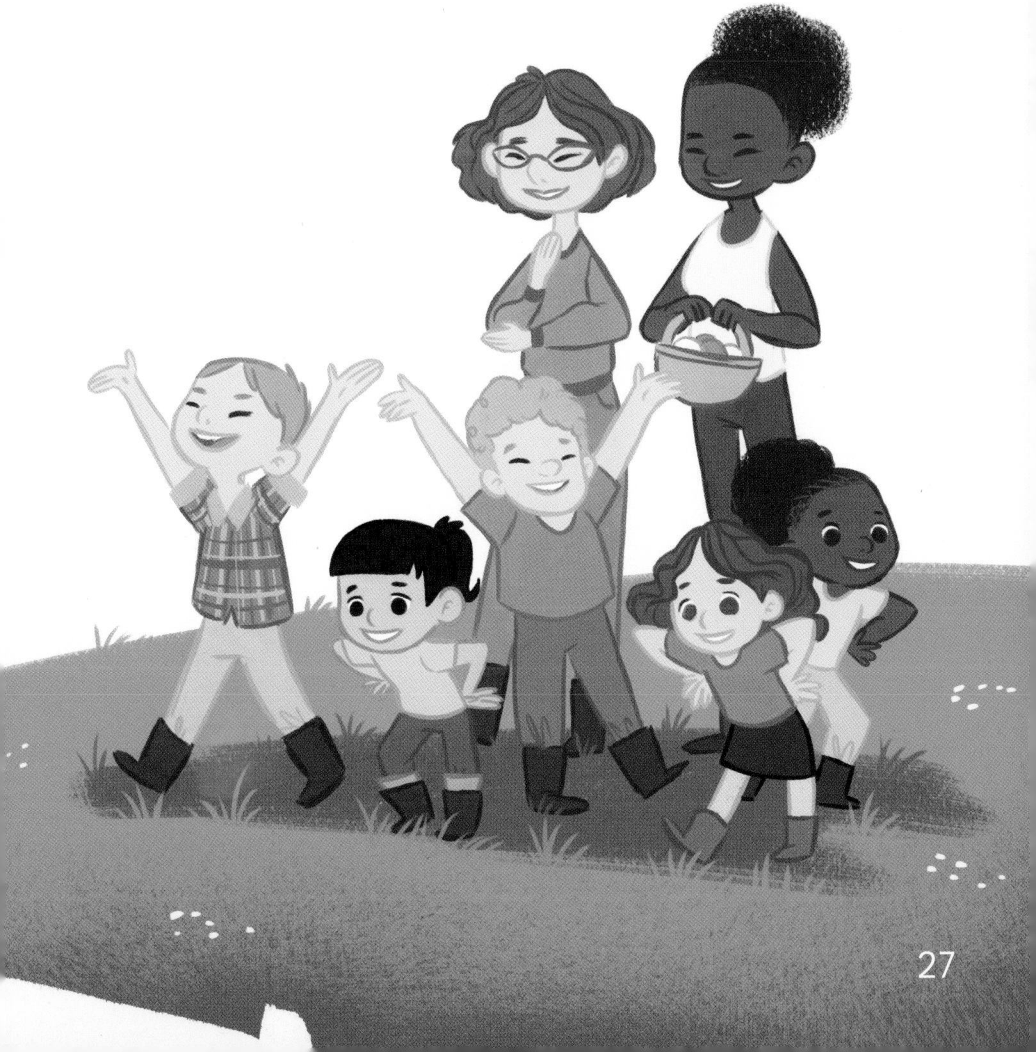

Chapter #5

Snack Time

"Next stop, the garden," Libby said.

"Tomatoes!" Xuni said. "My favorite!"

Everyone picked tomatoes. They picked lettuce, green onions, and carrots, too.

"I didn't know carrots grow below the ground," Alex said.

Libby nodded. "The part we eat is actually the root."

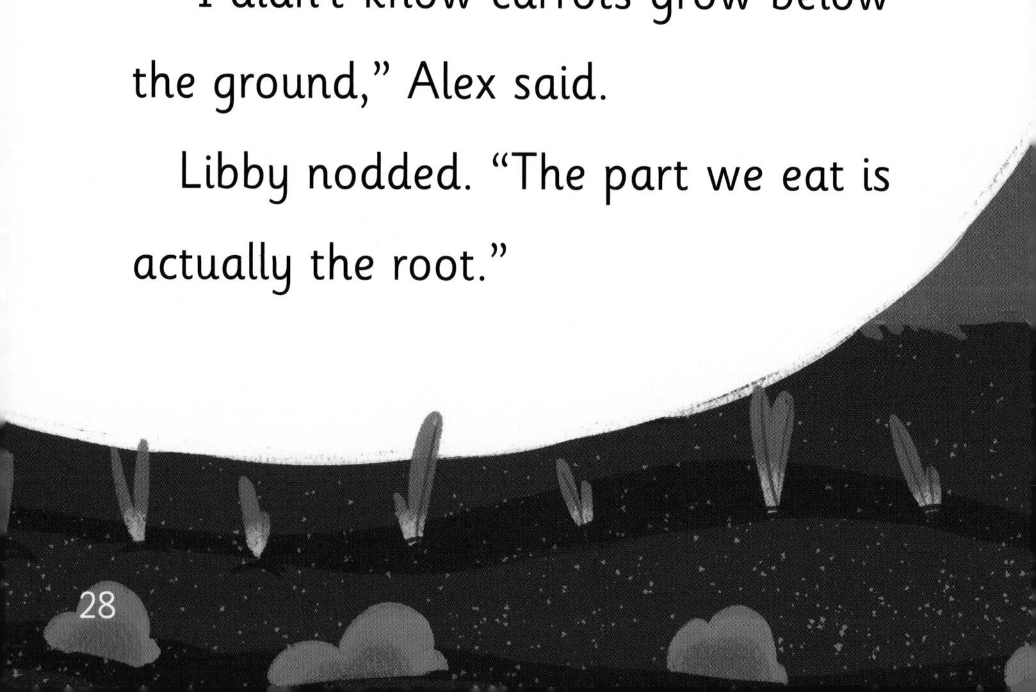

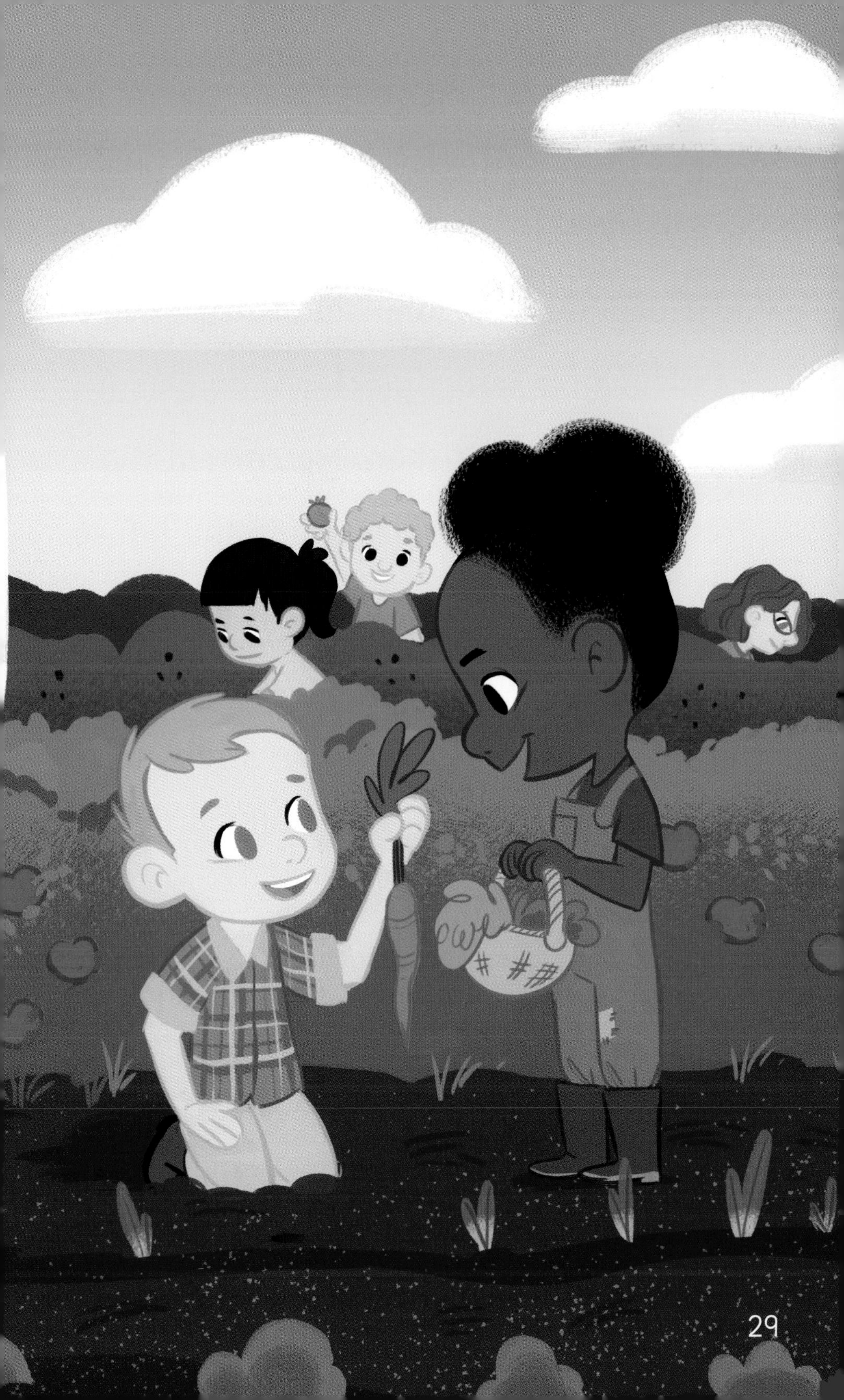

Clark noticed some plants with tiny yellow blooms. "What's this?" he asked.

"Cucumbers," Libby said. "My mom uses them to make pickles."

Dad came over then. He carried the fresh-picked vegetables inside the house.

After that, Libby and her friends took turns on the tire swing. And they played hide-and-seek in the tall cornstalks until Mom called, "It's snack time!"

"Come on!" Libby said.

Everyone followed her to a table piled with garden salad, carrot sticks, apple slices, and plump pickles. There was egg salad, too.

Alex asked, "Are those the eggs we gathered earlier?"

"Yep!" Libby smiled, proudly. "Everything you see was grown right here on our farm."

"That's cool!" Alex smiled, too.

Xuni crunched into a plump pickle. "These cucumbers are the best!"

"You know what else is the best?" Clark said.

"I know!" Alex said. "Libby, she's the best farm tour guide ever."